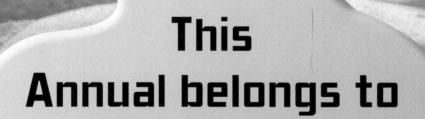

This
Annual belongs to

....

Fireman Sam
ANNUAL 2011

CONTENTS

EGMONT
We bring stories to life

Published in Great Britain 2010 by Egmont UK Limited
239 Kensington High Street, London W8 6SA

Text by Leah James and Laura Milne.
Design by Anthony Duke and Pritty Ramjee.
© 2010 Prism Art & Design Limited,
a HIT Entertainment company.
Based on an original idea by D.Gingell,
D. Jones and original characters created by R. M. J. Lee.

ISBN 978 1 4052 5368 0
10 9 8 7 6 5 4 3 2
Printed in Italy

WELCOME TO PONTYPANDY

Colour in the picture of Sam as neatly as you can.

Hello, I'm Fireman Sam. I hope you enjoy my new annual!

The items below are hidden in this annual. Count them up and write how many there are in the circles.

Have fun!

Answers on page 68.

PONTYPANDY RESCUE CREW

Name: Fireman Sam

Job: Firefighter

Likes: Inventing things, helping people, and looking after his nephew and niece, James and Sarah

Favourite saying: 'Great Fires of London!'

Drives: Jupiter, Pontypandy's fire engine, and the lifeboat, Neptune

Name: Station Officer Steele

Job: In charge of Pontypandy Fire Station

Likes: Safety checks, rules, training and giving orders

Dislikes: Rule-breakers

Favourite saying: 'Action Stations!'

Name: Elvis Cridlington

Job: Firefighter and fire station cook

Likes: Cooking, singing and looking cool

Favourite instrument: Electric guitar

Favourite saying: 'Great Balls of Fire!'

Name: Penny Morris

Job: Firefighter

Likes: Mechanics, hiking and rock climbing

Favourite saying: 'Go, girl, go!'

Drives: Venus the rescue tender, and the lifeboat, Neptune

Name: Tom Thomas

Job: Helicopter pilot for Mountain Rescue

Likes: Outdoor sports and rescuing animals in trouble

Favourite saying: 'G'day!'

Drives: Mountain rescue jeep and helicopter

PONTYPANDY PEOPLE

The Floods

Helen Flood is the local nurse. She drives her white rescue car to help out in emergencies.

Mike Flood is Pontypandy's handyman. He loves playing music with Elvis whenever he can.

Mandy Flood is best friends with Norman Price – they love going on adventures together!

The Joneses

Charlie Jones is Fireman Sam's brother. He is a fisherman and owns a green fishing boat.

Bronwyn Jones works in the fish shop and café, and loves to relax by meditating!

Sarah and James Jones are twins. They enjoy spending time with their Uncle Sam, and playing with Mandy and Norman.

The Prices

Dilys Price owns the Cut Price Supermarket in Pontypandy. She likes to gossip with her customers over a cup of tea.

Norman Price loves to play tricks and jokes on people. Everyone calls him Naughty Norman because he is always up to something!

Trevor Evans

Trevor Evans is Pontypandy's bus driver. He drives the children to school and likes to chat to Dilys. He loves the great outdoors and is a keen birdwatcher.

CRY WOLF

Sam is fitting a new fire alarm in Dilys' shop.

Thank you, Sam. I'll feel much safer now.

No problem, Dilys. I'll just test it.

Norman suddenly kicks his football and it knocks over a display of tins ...

Norman! Take that ball outside!

But it's too windy out there!

Fireman Sam tests the alarm, then turns it off.

BRRIINNNGGG!!!

If there's a fire, break the glass cover with the little hammer. But only if there's a fire!

Later that morning, Norman sneaks into the shop, dribbling his football. He accidentally kicks the ball too hard and it smashes the fire alarm glass.

BRRIINNNNGGG!!!!

Oh, crumbs!

Norman runs away. A few minutes later, Fireman Sam and Elvis arrive.

The alarm went off all by itself!

I can't see any smoke.

Fireman Sam and Elvis run into the shop. There is no fire. Fireman Sam sees the football and carries it outside.

I'd say this alarm didn't go off by itself.

You mean Norman? Oh, that boy!

13

Back inside Dilys' shop ...

I've hidden your football, Norman, because you set off the fire alarm.

What? No, it wasn't me! The alarm must be faulty.

Later, when he's alone, naughty Norman unscrews the glass on the fire alarm, and sets the alarm off! He quickly puts the glass back on.

BRRIINNNGGG!!!!

Fireman Sam and Elvis arrive at the shop again, in Jupiter. Fireman Sam turns the alarm off.

See, I told you it was faulty!

There's nothing wrong with that alarm, Norman. You set it off on purpose. Do you know the story of The Boy Who Cried Wolf?

Norman was told the story about the boy who kept pretending he'd seen a wolf. The boy would cry "Help! Wolf!" and all the villagers would come running. But one day a real wolf came and the boy cried out again, but this time nobody believed him and nobody came.

Did the wolf eat him up?

So they say …

SAFETY PATTERNS

Look at each line of pictures and say which safety item should come next. Draw the item in the space to complete the pattern.

1

2

3

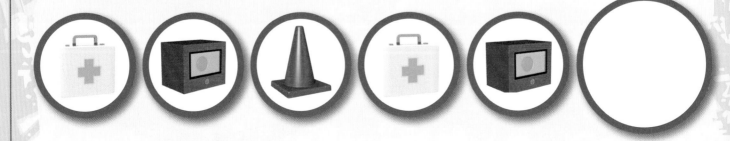

Answers on page 68.

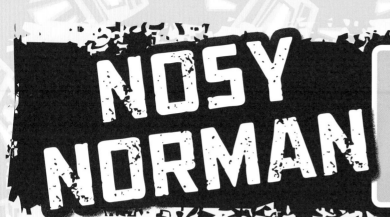

NOSY NORMAN

Norman is watching Fireman Sam and Penny through his binoculars. These four close-ups can all be seen in the big picture. Put a tick (✓) in the boxes when you've found them.

a b c d

THE ONE THAT GOT AWAY

Charlie had taken the twins and Norman fishing. The children were seeing who could catch the biggest fish. Suddenly, Norman leapt up.

There's a shark in the water!

I'll be right with you, Charlie!

Charlie explained that it wasn't a shark. It was a baby minke whale – a whale calf. He said that it was in trouble. "It's in very shallow water," said Charlie. "If it gets stuck on the beach it won't be able to get back in the water." Charlie called Tom for help.

"Tom thinks the whale calf has lost its mother," said Charlie. "We need to guide the calf back out to sea, and Tom is in the helicopter, searching for the mum."

Charlie steered the boat behind the calf, and it started swimming into deeper water. Just then, whilst Charlie was out on the deck, naughty Norman suddenly grabbed the wheel of the boat. The boat swerved towards the whale calf!

Arrgh!
Norman, what have you done?

There was a loud **THUD** and the boat rocked. The engine spluttered and died.

"It's the whale calf, it's hit us!" shouted Sarah. "And now the boat has a leak!"

Charlie set off an emergency flare. WHOOSH! A smoky jet shot up into the sky.

Tom was in his helicopter, still looking for the mother whale, when he saw the flare.

Charlie must be in trouble! I'll call Fireman Sam.

Fireman Sam and Penny got the alarm call and left the fire station in Venus, sirens blaring. They arrived at the boathouse, put on their sea rescue uniforms and climbed into Neptune, the lifeboat.

Help! *We're going to sink!*

Just keep calm, Norman.

Back on board his boat, Charlie was busy pumping out water. Norman was in a terrible flap.

Suddenly, James spotted Fireman
Sam and Penny. Neptune was soon
alongside Charlie's boat.

Fireman Sam carefully helped Sarah
and James into Neptune. Norman
agreed to stay with Charlie on his
boat and help pump the water out.

You stay and
help Charlie,
Norman.

Okay. I'll stay.

Thanks, Norman.
Well done.

We'll give you a tow, Charlie. We need to guide the calf back out to sea.

The boats guided the calf out to sea whilst Norman pumped water from Charlie's boat.

Suddenly, Tom appeared overhead in his helicopter. And there, in the sea, was the mother whale! The two whales greeted each other.

The calf has found its mum!

Yay!
Well done, Tom!

Tom flew away, and the whale calf bobbed up to the surface near the boat as if it was saying **thank you!**

Goodbye, little whale!

So who caught the largest fish?

Back on dry land, Charlie and the twins dropped Norman back home.

I'd say we all did. It was THI-IS BIG!

THE END

AMAZING NEPTUNE!

There's been a storm at sea and Charlie Jones has fallen overboard from his fishing boat! Can you show Penny the quickest way to find him in Neptune? Avoid the buoys as they will block your way!

START

Answer on page 68.

92

AT THE STATION

Colour in this picture of Pontypandy Fire Station. Can you draw Fireman Sam in the driveway?

THE WRONG SMELL

You can help read this story. Listen to the words and when you see a picture, say the name!

Radar

Helen

Mandy

Mike

Penny

Sam

Elvis

Tom

One day,  and are walking

in the mountains. But before long,

falls and twists her ankle.

bandages it up. They just start walking

again when the weather changes and the

friends get lost in thick fog.

 is worried when  has not

come home, and he calls the emergency

services.  ,  and

go to see  . They take  with

them.  gives  a jumper

which he thinks belongs to  . This is

for  to sniff, so that he can follow

the scent and help find the two friends.

But 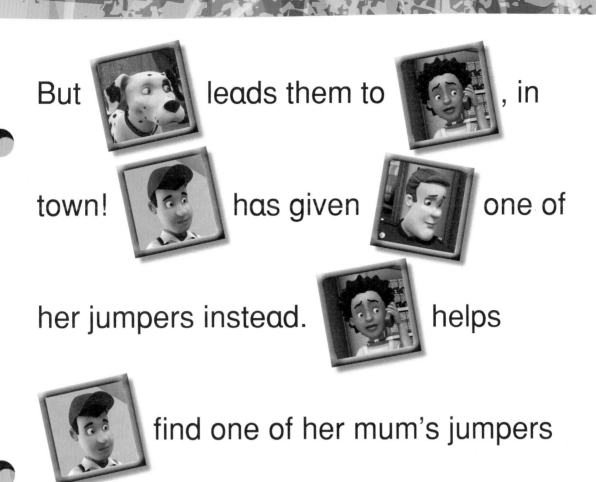 leads them to , in

town! has given one of

her jumpers instead. helps

find one of her mum's jumpers

and they hand it to  . "This is

definitely Mum's!" says  .

 sniffs the jumper, and the

rescuers are ready to go.

The rescue party all climb into Venus and

they drive into the mountains. It is dark and

foggy outside, but  and

have torches.  sniffs the air and

goes running off. Everybody follows him,

and they soon hear  call out.

"Over here!"

she says.

The rescue party have found  and

 !  is limping, but she is

okay.  and  take the two

friends back to the fire station.

rests her ankle. "Thank you,  !"

she says. "And thank you,  ."

"I will definitely take a nurse with me every

time I go hiking!" she laughs.

THE END

RACE TO THE TOP

Tom and Penny have gone for a hike on Pontypandy Mountain and it's turned into a race! Who will reach the top first?

Find short cut. Go forward 2 spaces.

How to play

You will need: a dice and a counter for each player.

• This is a game for 2 players. Decide who will be Penny and who will be Tom.

• Place the counters on the START square, then throw the dice and move around the board.

• Follow the instructions as you go, and if you land on a space with rocks on it, miss a turn.

• If you land on a space with a map, take a shortcut and zoom ahead by taking an extra turn.

• The first player to reach the FINISH is the winner!

START

FINISH

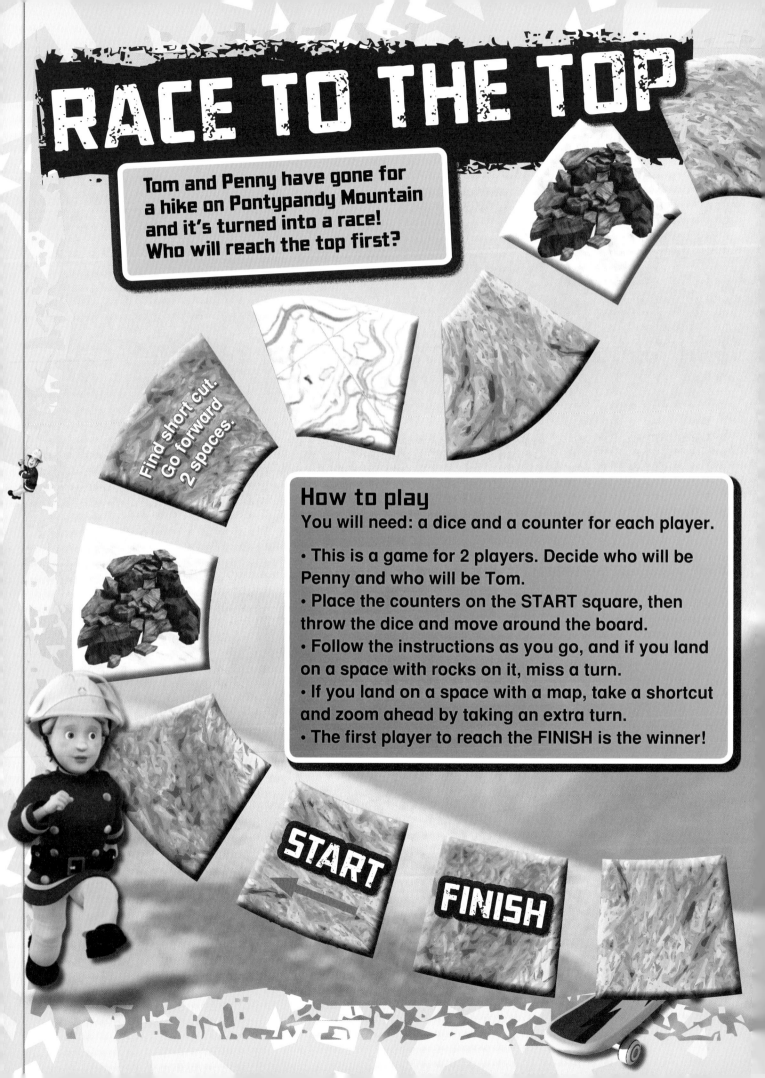

Stop for sandwich.
Go back 1 space.

Have a rest.
Miss a go.

35

DANGER!

Can you spot danger like a Pontypandy rescue hero? Circle the dangerous things in these pictures. Can you say why they could cause an emergency? Check your answers on page 68.

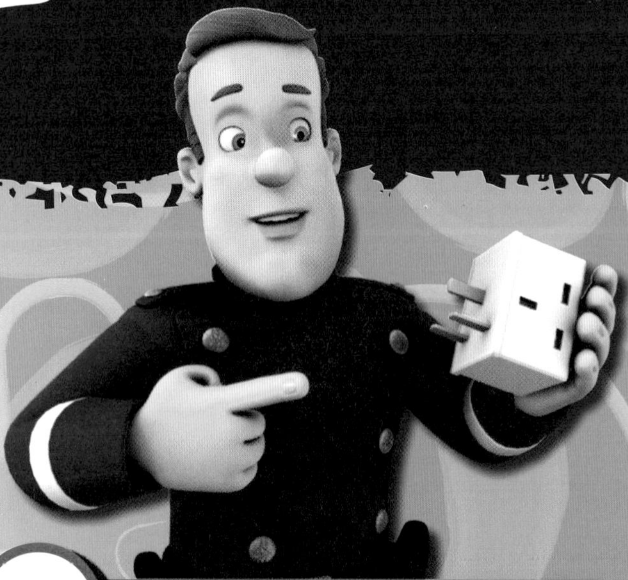

2

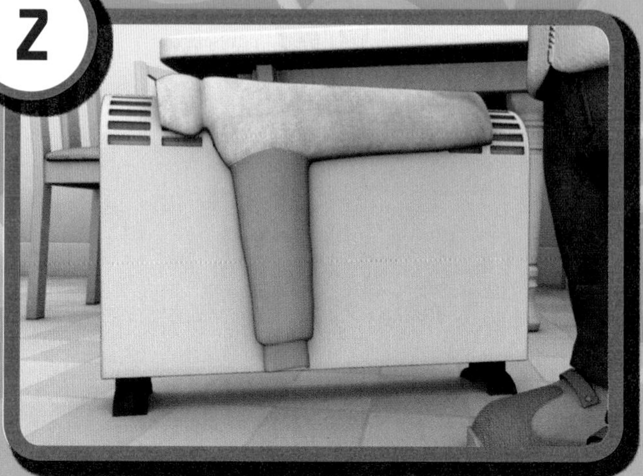

1

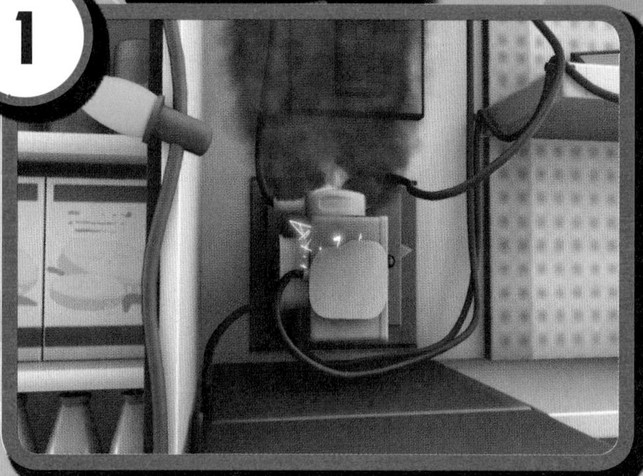

4

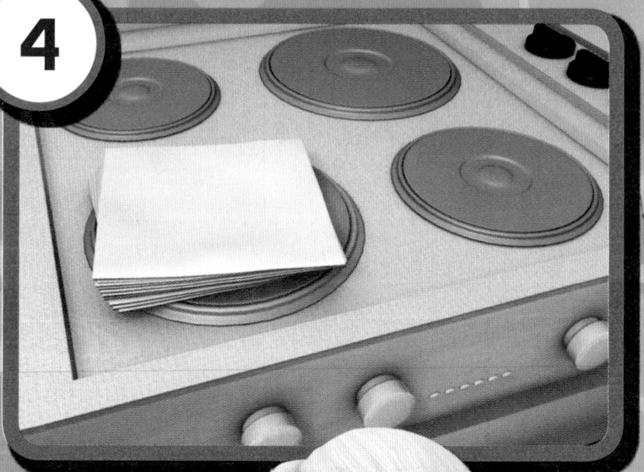

3

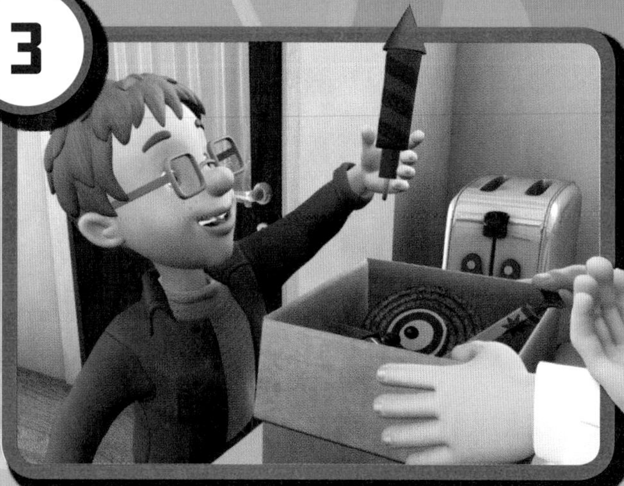

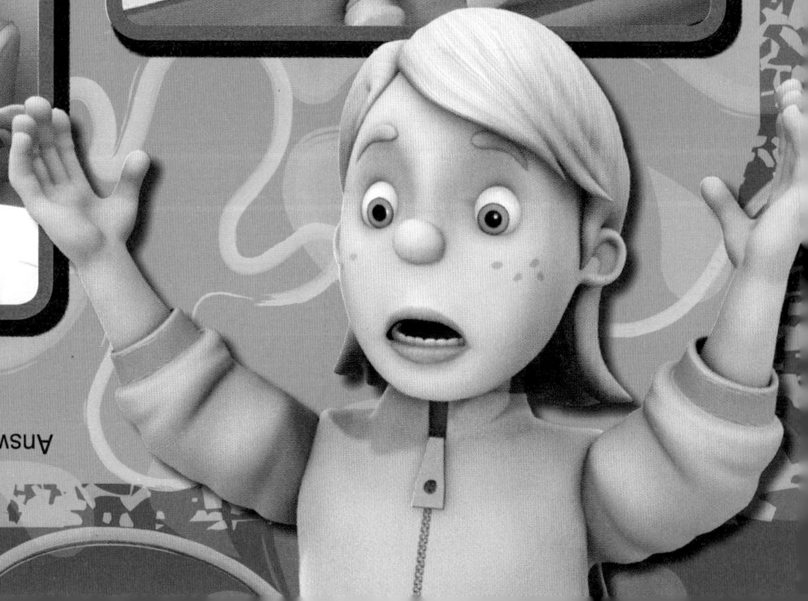

Answers on page 68.

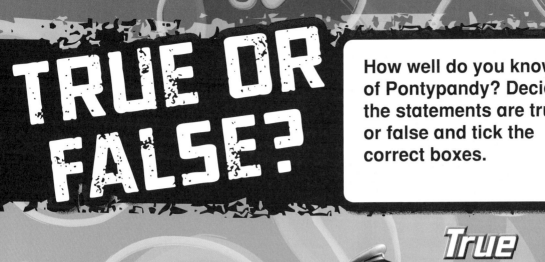

TRUE OR FALSE?

How well do you know the people of Pontypandy? Decide if the statements are true or false and tick the correct boxes.

True   **False**

1. Trevor drives the school bus

2. Tom comes from Australia

3. Fireman Sam has a grey moustache

4. The firefighters wear green helmets

5. Neptune is a lifeboat

6. James is Dilys' son

Answers on page 68.

37

ALARM ON THE BEACH

You can help read this story. Listen to the words and when you see a picture, say the name!

Sam

Penny

Sarah

James

Mandy

Elvis

One warm and sunny day, ,

 and  are playing on the

beach. After a little while,  comes

across a wooden crate washed up on the

beach. "There may be treasure inside it!"

she says excitedly.

Meanwhile,  has gone to wake up

 at his home.  has slept in!

"You're late for work again," says .

"Sorry," says . "I find it hard to

wake up in the morning." The two of them

drive away in Jupiter.

On the beach,  ,  and

 are trying to open the crate.

Suddenly, the heavy crate topples onto

 and traps his legs. He is stuck,

and there is a strange ticking noise coming

from the crate!  runs to find a

phone and she calls the fire brigade.

 and  quickly arrive in

Jupiter.  is out at sea, in Neptune.

She radios  to tell him where on

the beach the children are. The firefighters

soon find  and lift the crate off him.

"Hooray, I'm out! Thank you!" he says.

 is safe, but the crate is still ticking!

 carefully opens the crate and

peers inside. "The crate is full of alarm

clocks," he laughs. He hands a clock to

 . "Thanks ," says  .

"I need one of these to help wake me up in

the morning!"

THE END

SPOT THE DIFFERENCE

Fireman Sam and Station Officer Steele are arriving back at the fire station.

1

These pictures look the same but 5 things
are different in picture 2.

Circle the differences as you spot them.

Z

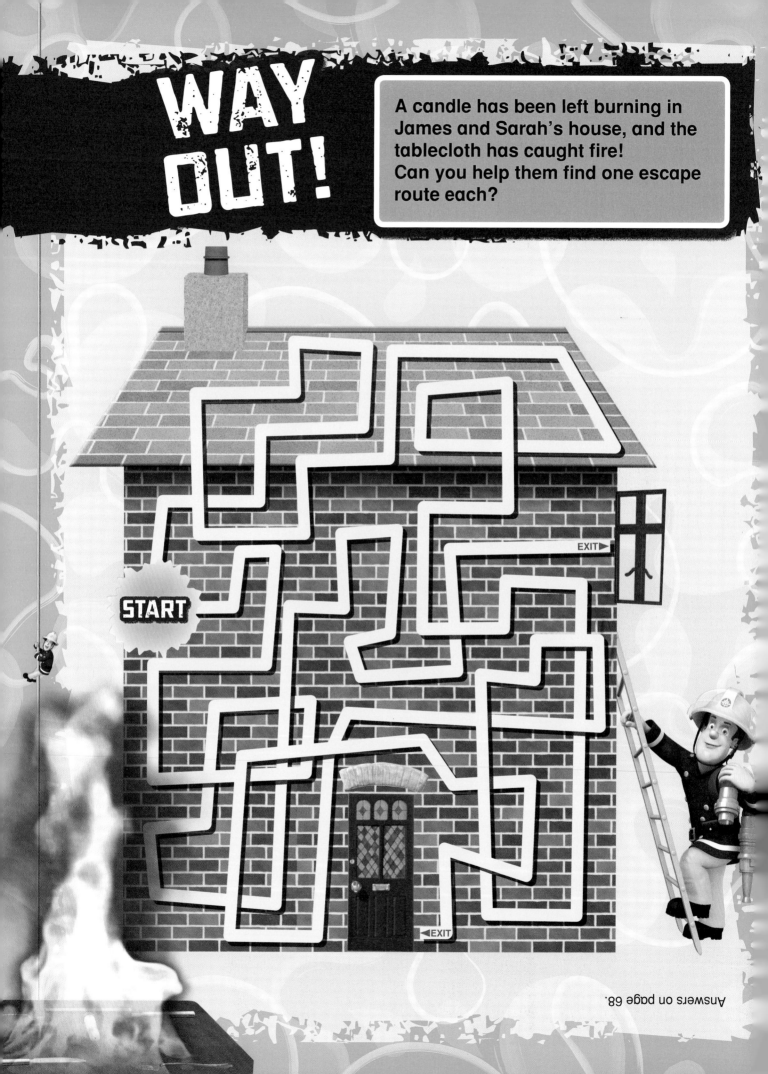

WAY OUT!

A candle has been left burning in James and Sarah's house, and the tablecloth has caught fire!
Can you help them find one escape route each?

START

EXIT ▶

◀ EXIT

Answers on page 68.

ESCAPE ROUTE

Now that you've led James and Sarah to safety, can you draw a picture of your own house and draw a path to safety? Ask a grown-up to help you practise your escape route.

re's an idea to help you: the best escape route the normal way in and out of your house!

STICKY SITUATION

One warm sunny morning, Norman is walking around Pontypandy. He is listening to music on his MP3 player with his headphones on.

Norman is just about to step out in front of Trevor's bus. Luckily, Fireman Sam sees him and pulls him back.

PONTYPANDY

SCREECH!!!

You can't hear the cars coming.

Fireman Sam tells Norman that crossing the road with head-phones on is very dangerous.

"Sorry, Sam," says Norman. "I was listening to my new MP3 player. I got it for my birthday."

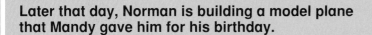

Later that day, Norman is building a model plane that Mandy gave him for his birthday.

Mandy notices that Norman has put his magnifying glass on a piece of card, and the sun is shining through it.

"Careful, Norman!" says Mandy. "The glass is in the sun."

You could start a fire!

But Norman is more concerned with his plane. He runs downstairs to find some strong glue.

This sticks anything and lasts forever!

If you get it on your hands, you could get stuck to anything.

But Norman loses his temper and snaps at Mandy. Poor Mandy gets upset, and she leaves.

Oh!

Back upstairs, the magnifying glass is in the sun again, and it's shining on the model's instructions. They start to smoulder.

Soon, a fire has started. Norman jumps and accidentally squirts some of the really strong glue on his hands.

He opens his bedroom door and calls for his mum.

MAM!

50

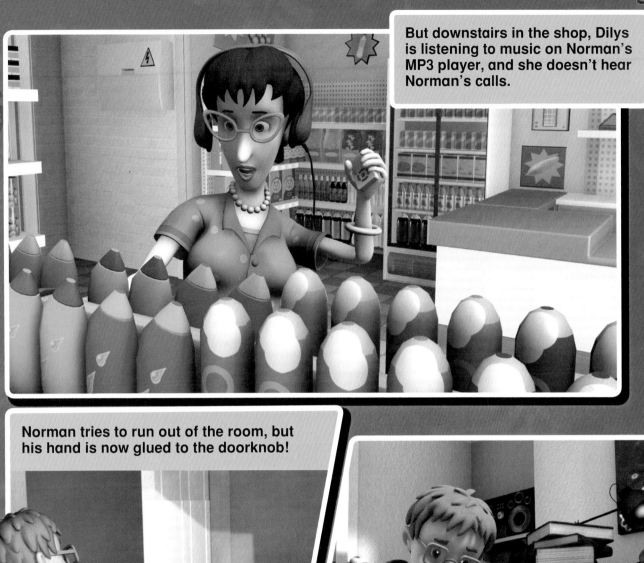

But downstairs in the shop, Dilys is listening to music on Norman's MP3 player, and she doesn't hear Norman's calls.

Norman tries to run out of the room, but his hand is now glued to the doorknob!

Norman thinks hard. He just manages to reach one of his books, and he throws it at the model plane. The burning model is knocked out of the window ... into the path of Mike Flood who's driving his van below!

Mike stops the van and looks up to see smoke coming from Norman's room. He quickly calls the Pontypandy Fire Station on his mobile phone.

Whoa! Where did that come from?

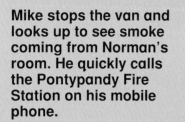

It isn't long before Fireman Sam, Penny and Elvis arrive at the scene. Dilys still has the headphones on, and is shocked to see Fireman Sam and Penny burst through the shop, dragging a hose! Elvis tells her about the fire upstairs.

Fireman Sam and Penny find Norman upstairs. Seeing that Norman is glued to the door, Fireman Sam says that the whole door will quickly have to be taken off its hinges!

Fireman Sam soon puts the fire out, and everybody is safe. Penny takes Norman outside – still stuck to the door! She asks Dilys to find some nail varnish remover which will help unstick Norman's hand.

Thanks, Penny. If only I hadn't been wearing those headphones!

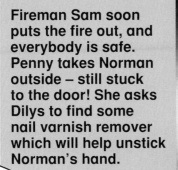

Later on, back inside the shop, Mike offers to help Norman make a new model plane.

"Well," says Fireman Sam, "It's time to head back to the station now, Elvis."

But Elvis can't hear him – he's too busy bopping away to a tune on Norman's MP3 player!

FOLLOW THE STORY

Now you've read Sticky Situation, can you remember what happened? Put the pictures in order by writing the letters in the boxes.

a

b

c

d

1

2

3

4

Answers on page 68.

NEE NAH!

Sam is driving by in Jupiter! Colour in the picture, using the colour code to help you.

ACTION STATIONS

Draw a line to match each character to their shadow.

Answers on page 68.

SAM SEARCH!

How many times can you find the name Sam in this word square, reading across or down?

Then, how many pictures of Sam can you count below?

f	s	a	m
s	a	m	i
a	m	r	e
m	s	a	m

TOWERING INFERNO

Norman is arguing in the street with Mandy! They are debating who is the best at hiding in Pontypandy.

Sarah stands between Norman and Mandy, to calm them down.

Let's see who is best at hiding!

James says they will have a challenge to see whether it is Norman or Mandy who is best at hiding! James and Sarah shut their eyes and start counting, whilst Norman and Mandy run off to hide.

Over at the Pontypandy Fire Station, the fire officers are getting ready for a training session. They are going to practise rescuing someone from a fire in the training tower. They will rescue a dummy called Dolly!

She looks lovely up there!

Dolly is carried up to the top of the training tower, and Fireman Sam places the material to start the fire at the bottom of the tower. Elvis thinks Dolly is beautiful!

Meanwhile, down at the harbour, Mandy has crept onboard Charlie's fishing boat. It is moored at the quay. Mandy hides behind some lobster pots.

James and Sarah search the streets of Pontypandy, looking for Norman and Mandy. Then they walk down to the beach. James looks through his binoculars and spots his dad's fishing boat at sea. He sees that Mandy is on the boat!

Charlie didn't know Mandy was on his boat when he left the quay, but he discovers her when they're out at sea. Mandy isn't feeling very well.

Hey, Mandy's on Dad's boat!

Urrrgh ...
I'm seasick ...

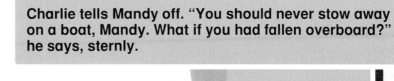

Charlie tells Mandy off. "You should never stow away on a boat, Mandy. What if you had fallen overboard?" he says, sternly.

Charlie docks his boat back at the quay. James and Sarah are there to meet Mandy. "It looks like Norman has won the hiding challenge, then!" says James.

The children run off to look for Norman. They bump into Dilys outside the supermarket. She is worried that Norman is still missing. She decides to call the Pontypandy Fire Service.

Fireman Sam puts a call through to Tom Thomas. Tom and Mandy fly up into the sky in the helicopter, to look for Norman.

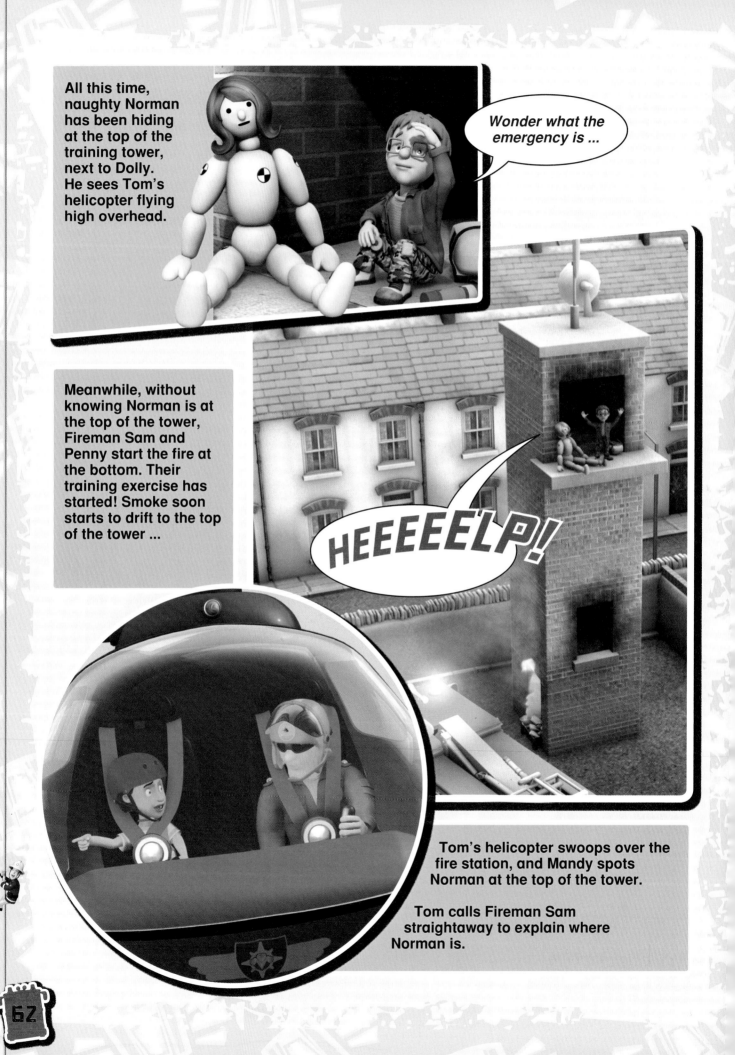

All this time, naughty Norman has been hiding at the top of the training tower, next to Dolly. He sees Tom's helicopter flying high overhead.

Wonder what the emergency is ...

Meanwhile, without knowing Norman is at the top of the tower, Fireman Sam and Penny start the fire at the bottom. Their training exercise has started! Smoke soon starts to drift to the top of the tower ...

HEEEEELP!

Tom's helicopter swoops over the fire station, and Mandy spots Norman at the top of the tower.

Tom calls Fireman Sam straightaway to explain where Norman is.

Fireman Sam tells Elvis to put out the fire at the bottom of the tower. Meanwhile, Fireman Sam carefully climbs Jupiter's ladder so that he can reach Norman.

Fireman Sam carries Norman carefully onto the ladder, and brings him safely back down to the ground. Everybody cheers when Norman has been rescued, but Station Officer Steele tells him off for hiding at the fire station.

As Dilys marches Norman back home, Elvis spots Dolly who has also been rescued from the fire. He is so happy that she is safe!

You really are a hero, Sam!

THE END

MISCHIEF MAKER

Only 2 of these pictures of Norman playing superhero are exactly the same. Can you see which two they are?

a

b

c

d

e

Answers on page 68.

LOST PROPERTY

Draw a line to match each person to their property.

Tom

Dilys

Norman

Elvis

Penny

(a)

(b)

(c)

(d)

(e)

Answers on page 68.

65

FIRE SAFETY

Fireman Sam is giving a safety lesson to help you.

Ask a grown-up:

To fit (and test) smoke alarms in your home.

How you could all safely get out of the house, if there was a fire.

How to dial 999.

How to tell someone where you live.

ANSWERS

Page 7 WELCOME TO PONTYPANDY

Skateboard – 3 times, on pages 11, 34 and 55

Cup – 3 times, on pages 8, 47, 64

Torch – 2 times, on pages 10 and 35

Firework – 3 times, on pages 11, 26 and 57

Page 18 SAFETY PATTERNS

1 –   2 – 3 –

Page 26 AMAZING NEPTUNE!

Page 36 DANGER!

1 – A socket with too many plugs in it could cause a fire.

2 – Drying or warming clothes on a heater could cause a fire.

3 – It is dangerous for children to touch or play with fireworks.

4 – Objects left on a hot cooker could cause a fire.

Page 37 TRUE OR FALSE?

1 – True 2 – True 3 – False 4 – False
5 – True 6 – False.

Pages 44 and 45 SPOT THE DIFFERENCE

Page 46 WAY OUT!

Page 54 FOLLOW THE STORY

1 – c, 2 – d, 3 – b, 4 – a

Page 56 ACTION STATIONS

1 – d, 2 – a, 3 – e, 4 – b, 5 – c

Page 57 SAM SEARCH!

Sam appears 5 times in the word square. There are 5 pictures of Fireman Sam.

Page 64 MISCHIEF MAKER

Pictures a and d are exactly the same.

Page 65 LOST PROPERTY

Tom – c, Dilys – d, Norman – e, Elvis – a, Penny – b

Fireman Sam™

Don't miss Fireman Sam in his own magazine! Packed full of stories, posters and activities.

FREE GIFT WITH EVERY ISSUE!

Use your brightest crayons or pens to colour in this picture.

ON SALE EVERY 4 WEEKS!

On sale in all good newsagents and supermarkets now!